Buying His Omega

Galactic Alphas, Volume 2

Juno Wells

Published by Publishers' Portal, 2020.

Blurb

ALPHA RYDER ISN'T LOOKING for an Omega, but when he sees Daisy being auctioned to the highest bidder, he can't resist bidding on her. Before he knows it, he's spent a year's earnings to buy the Omega. He offers her the choice of returning home, but she needs to mate desperately. Barely managing to resist claiming her, he's shocked when she pulls him into a desperate rescue attempt to save her fellow Omega, who was also sold. Pursuing the buyers, Ryder sees the promise and possibility of a future with his Omega, but does Daisy even want such a thing, or will she choose her cloistered life at the Omega convent over being claimed by an Alpha?

Chapter One

DAISY COULDN'T SPEAK Klinok, and if the aliens spoke any English, they didn't reveal it. They were talking and gesticulating among themselves as she observed from the clear box in which they had kept her since stealing her from her home planet along with her friend last week.

Thinking of her, she glanced over to Azaria's box, finding her friend didn't appear as fearful of whatever was happening, but Daisy knew Azaria was probably feeling it as well. She was more stoic and naturally able to hide her emotions better than Daisy. She knew her friend well enough, having grown up with her most of her life, to guess Azaria was as terrified as she was.

Azaria looked at her, and their gazes locked. They were able to communicate through their boxes, and Daisy considered that one small kindness from the aliens. The Klinoks also made sure they were fed regularly, but it was difficult to be grateful for the smallest of courtesies when they had attacked Paladin and dragged the two women from their home before the rest of the sisters at the Omega convent stopped the invasion.

"Whatever happens, you'll be okay." Azaria gave her an encouraging smile.

Daisy shook her head, fear nearly getting the best of her. "I don't see how. They're going to sell us. We'll be separated and never allowed to return home." Her eyes welled with tears, and she sniffed.

"You must be strong, Daisy. You're stronger than you believe, so whatever happens, you must keep your eyes open and wait for an opportunity to escape."

Daisy nodded, trying to look more confident in the idea. It was mainly for Azaria's benefit though. She didn't think she had it in her to survive this ordeal, let alone find a way to escape an Alpha or a group of Alphas. Since she didn't speak Klinok, she couldn't be certain of their intention, but they'd spent all morning prepping the two of them, including washing them through the box, and she had a feeling they were being put on display.

Omegas knew the risk of being sold to a group of selfish Alphas who would share her during her estrus with no intention of claiming her as a mate or caring for her properly. Daisy had always hoped it was an old wives' tale passed among the sisters at the convent, but now she suspected there was far more truth to it than she'd been aware.

Whatever the two Klinoks had been discussing, they seemed to have settled it now. The larger one—which was difficult to discern, since they were a lumbering race at least twice the size of Daisy and Azaria, with gnarled gray or brown skin, depending on the individual Klinok—moved over to Azaria's cage.

Daisy trembled as the smaller one approached hers, and he had some kind of tube in his hands. She watched with alarm as he pushed it into the airlock atop of the box. It was how they had distributed the cleaning chemicals earlier before sucking them through again with a vacuum system.

She trembled again, recalling how frantic she had been the first day of her captivity, to the point where she'd been panicking and trying to break through the impenetrable clear box. One of those Klinoks had approached and put in a similar chemical that had turned out to be a gas to put her to sleep. She was expecting the same thing, and she did her best to hold her breath while the pale lavender mist filtered in through the box, but she was eventually forced to breathe.

At first, she experienced no change, so she assumed it must be something different from the sedative they had given her the first day. That had acted almost immediately, instantly loosening her muscles and putting her to sleep in under a minute. She appeared unchanged, and she was confused. Glancing over to Azaria, her friend seemed to be in a similar state. She was outwardly as calm as she had been before they administered whatever was in the tubes.

There was an itching sensation settling over her body, and Daisy started scratching through the thin layer of the jumpsuit they had given her to wear after taking the heavier robes she wore at the convent. Even then, when they had insisted she change clothes on her first day, there had been an air of apathy about them. Daisy had never felt sexually threatened by the Klinoks, but she was still deathly afraid of them and their intentions.

Azaria was starting to squirm as well, and she was sweating suddenly. Daisy lifted an arm to wipe her brow as she realized she was also perspiring heavily. The itching sensation had turned to a burning, and she was shocked to feel a sudden jolt of arousal in her core. She shifted, needing something, though she'd never experienced anything like this before.

She moved her hand between her legs, cupping the heat there, trying to provide some kind of relief with the press of friction. It did little to relieve her, and she writhed and moaned, suddenly burning up. She must be running a raging fever, and she realized she was entering estrus.

Daisy had been through it before, but a blunted version. The Omegas at the convent took a low-dose suppressant that allowed them to have natural cycles and function without succumbing to the wild throes of estrus. The few she had endured since puberty had been much milder than this.

They sometimes required sequestering herself to ride out the worst of it with a couple of her favorite toys, but she'd never experienced this aching burn of desire before. If she didn't have an Alpha soon, she was going to die. She just knew it, and she was still aware enough to realize the fever burning through her could permanently damage her physically if she didn't find respite.

One of the Klinoks approached, heaving her box onto a wheeled stand with seemingly no effort at all. Daisy put her palm to the glass, and

Azaria did the same. Her friend appeared to be struggling as much as she was, though Azaria still managed a strong smile, and her voice sounded confident. "Be brave and survive, Daisy."

Daisy whimpered as she was wheeled from view of her friend, starting to lose herself in the heat of estrus without any cognizance of what was happening. She was vaguely aware of being trundled onto a platform, and as she looked around, she saw a number of human Alphas among the crowd, along with a mix of a few other aliens. She didn't know if any other races had the same affinity for Omegas human Alphas had, and she was startled to realize she didn't care who bought her as long as they eased this burning aching inside.

She whimpered at the thought, closing her eyes and trying to summon her strength. She'd never realized just how overwhelming estrus could be, and while she was disgusted at her lack of willpower, she was craving an Alpha even more.

She opened her eyes, fighting against the urges inside her, and her gaze locked with a tall Alpha near the front. He had white-blond hair, a neatly trimmed beard, and the impressive size and bulging muscles that identified him as an Alpha even though she couldn't smell his pheromones with the box filtering out any scent.

She looked harder at him, feeling herself melt inside. She pressed her palms to the glass, mouthing, "Alpha." She wanted him more than anything in the world, but the pain and burning inside was too much for her. She closed her eyes as she collapsed to the floor, writhing in search of relief.

Chapter Two

RYDER STRANG DIDN'T often deal with the Klinok, since he knew they sold all sorts of contraband on their market ships. The ships changed locations on a frequent basis to avoid Coalition enforcers, but since he'd found himself in range of one, it had seemed as good a place as any to sell the rathium bars he had been smuggling. Since he hadn't acquired them through strictly legal means, and he certainly had no permit to be carrying the quantity he had aboard in his secret hold, he was happy to be rid of them as quickly as possible.

He'd finished his business, selling the rathium bars for a tidy profit in under eighteen minutes, and his credit account felt much heavier now, though it was all digital. He was heading back to the *Remedy*, his sweet little freighter that he'd paid for himself through hard work, even if it hadn't all been legitimate and aboveboard Coalition-approved labor.

As he was moving through the crowd, he realized there were several Alphas gathered together. It wasn't unusual to see so many humans, since his race had spread practically to every part of the galaxy, but it was startling enough to see so many Alphas together that it caught his attention. He moved closer, disgust soon filling him when he saw a notice announcing it was an auction selling beings. The headline highlighted two Omegas would be up for sale.

Ryder shuddered at the thought. He'd never been lucky enough to encounter an Omega before who wasn't already mated to an Alpha, but he couldn't imagine being so desperate for the experience that he would buy and enslave one. As an Alpha, he viewed it as his duty to protect any Omega who fell under his care and taking away her choice to be with him certainly didn't mean taking care of her in his eyes.

He started to turn away in revulsion, wishing he could find a way to stop this travesty but knowing he was vastly outnumbered, when something made him look back. He couldn't control his feet as he moved closer, pushing atthe crowd and receiving some pushback that had him growling his way through.

His gaze locked with the pretty little Omega on the stage before him. She had ebony skin, thick curly hair, and a pleasing roundness to her frame that had his Alpha sitting up and taking notice. He was nearly overwhelmed with the urge to claim her, and he hadn't even smelled her scent yet, since the box she was trapped in filtered out her pheromones and prevented a frenzy.

As the emcee stepped forward, he couldn't look away from her. She mouthed the word Alpha, and his own lips formed, "Omega," unconsciously. He took another step forward as the emcee started the bidding with the announcement this Omega and the other one waiting to be bid on had both been given enhancers, so they were already in estrus and immediately prepared for breeding. That sent a roar of excitement through the crowd, and even Ryder shivered with pleasure at the thought, though he hated the instinctive reaction that being an Alpha near an Omega in estrus brought about.

He had every intention of walking away. He didn't agree with what was happening, but the more he stared at the suffering Omega, the more he was determined to save her. She was clearly writhing in pain and need, and he was sure any of the other Alphas in the room who got her wouldn't hesitate to use her however they chose. Her pleasure and care would be the last thing they'd worry about after paying for her.

The thought was abhorrent, and before he knew it, he was raising his hand to bid. It was a tense few minutes, and he started to sweat as the rathium proceeds dwindled. Before he knew it, he'd spent almost a year of expenses, but he was the winner of the pretty Omega in the box. He moved forward to pay, going to the bursar at the edge of the crowd, who told him she would be delivered to his ship within the next half-hour.

"Make it ten minutes," he said with all the anger he could display. He wasn't about to have the poor Omega suffer even longer than necessary.

The bursar, a pale Beta male, started to sweat. "I'll see what I can do...Captain Strang." He looked down at the reader to acquire Ryder's name before handing back his card.

Still uneasy about his actions, and worried about the Omega, Ryder moved through the crowd again. He stormed away from the area of the auction, heading back to his ship. He'd only gone a couple of corridors when he realized he was being followed. It set his teeth on edge, and a low growl emitted from his throat.

He reached for the laser pistol at his hip, grasping it as he spun around to face whomever was stalking him. He was unsurprised to find two Alphas, and they likely planned to set upon him, maybe even kill him, for an opportunity to steal his Omega.

The thought unleashed a protective instinct he'd never experienced before. He was naturally nurturing and caring toward those who were weaker, since that was his biological imperative, but this was a new kind of intensity and need to protect. He shot one of them as the other Alpha ran toward him, dropping the human to the floor.

He didn't have time to turn his gun on the other before the second Alpha plowed into him. Ryder went with the attack, rolling in midair so he was the one who landed on top. He pounded his fists into the Alpha's face several times until the body went slack beneath him. He didn't know or care if he'd killed him. To be so disreputable as to attack and try to steal his Omega warranted no concern for the fate of the two Alphas who had acted so dishonorably. They were the kind who had successfully overcome the biological imperative to protect, instead embracing their own selfish urges and desires.

He stood up, leaving the trash behind him. Since the Klinok market ship wasn't exactly an aboveboard establishment, he doubted they would be the only two bodies left behind that day. The Klinoks likely had some way to deal with disposal, and it was certainly something that would never see the light of day in a Coalition report. It was truly a lawless zone, and he knew from previous experience the Klinoks didn't care what you did as long as you paid for the purchases they offered.

He broke into a sprint, covering the rest of the distance to his ship and entering through the airlock. He was inside and waiting when two Klinoks showed up eventually, far later than ten minutes. He thought about unleashing his anger on them at making her suffer that much longer, but when he looked at the Omega, all his concern was for her. He gestured for them to bring her inside through the airlock. As soon as she was safely secured, he said, "Get out."

The Klinoks might not speak his language, but they clearly understood his intent. They lumbered through the airlock, having to bend down to clear the doorway, and he sealed the ship behind them.

He turned to her, concern and desire warring inside him. He wanted more than anything to claim her, and he hadn't even smelled her pheromones yet. Instead, he clung to his principles, which told him it wasn't right to impose his will upon her.

He approached cautiously as she clawed at the box, her desperation even higher than it was when he'd bought her. He put his palm against the clear box, and she did the same. "Alpha, please."

At least she could communicate through the box. He was grateful for that. "What's your name?"

"Alpha." She was practically mewling now.

"I need to know your name, honey." He made his voice firm, hoping she would respond to that.

Her gaze was unfocused, and she looked a little dazed, but her dark eyes focused on him eventually, and he was entranced by the rich brown shade. She licked her lips in an enticing fashion as she said, "Daisy."

The way she drew out each syllable made him shiver, and his arousal raised another notch. His cock was straining against the confines of his pants, and it took every ounce of willpower he had to say, "I can help you. If you don't want to mate to end the estrus, you can stay in the box until

I can find you some suppressant. That should ease your suffering within an hour or so. Is that what you want, Daisy?"

"I want you, Alpha. I need you. Please."

He trembled, feeling himself on the edge of giving in. "You don't even know me, honey. I want to make sure you get a choice in all this. Do you think you can wait a few hours for relief?"

She whimpered, and her lower lip, which was lusciously full and completely bite-able, extended in a pouting fashion. "It hurts, Alpha. Help me."

It was his biological imperative to do just that, but there was more to it than acting on instinct. He wanted to protect her and take away her suffering, but Ryder was drawn to the Omega herself. He'd never really considered he'd have the opportunity or the option of having an Omega of his own, having figured it was a pipe dream due to the rarity of them, along with his lack of a stable lifestyle that might attract the typical mate.

Now that she was before him, he couldn't resist the temptation any longer. He pressed his palm to the box, pleased to find they had calibrated it to respond to his biometrics before leaving it, and the walls fell downward with a slight clattering sound. Her scent hit him then, and Ryder was completely lost.

As she rushed him, jumping into his arms, he caught her and held her tightly against him before burying his mouth against her throat, nuzzling her scent gland and licking frantically. She was the one in estrus, but he was suddenly close to rutting, and he was certain he wouldn't be able to hold back the urge. He would have to remember to be careful with her, to ensure she enjoyed the experience, but he wasn't certain how he would do so as his mind hazed over with animalistic passion, the Alpha inside roaring its pleasure at finding an Omega to breed.

Chapter Three

HE SMELLED SO GOOD, and she hurt so much that Daisy couldn't resist. She launched herself into the Alpha's arms, throwing back her head as he started nuzzling her scent gland. She writhed against him, rubbing her sheath against his stomach as she sought relief. At some point during her estrus, she must have ripped off the jumpsuit the Klinok had given her, because she was completely naked.

He wasn't, and she found that displeasing. She started to pull at his uniform, and he growled in approval. When he set her down, she immediately reached for him again, but one stern look from him and another growl of warning had her freezing. Even in the throes of this intense estrus, the Omega in her responded to the Alpha in him.

Part of her hated that weakness, but it wasn't the rational part of her in charge now, and that concern soon faded. Once the Alpha in front of her had removed his armor and flight suit, he took her back into his arms. She went eagerly, wrapping her thighs around his waist as she sought out his thick cock, rubbing her slit against it. Slick poured from her, drenching both of them, and he moaned. She wanted nothing more than to have him inside her, and she started to take him.

"Slow down, Daisy." He seemed to have trouble getting out those words as he carried her to the captain's chair nearby. He sat down, and this allowed her far better positioning, perched on his lap as she was.

When she rubbed against him again, he moaned, and he didn't fight this time as she reached for his shaft to line it up with her opening and take him inside. There was a moment of intense pain, and his eyes widened.

"Were you a virgin?" He sounded appalled at the thought.

Daisy had no time for conversation or clear thought. She only wanted to feel, and with the fever burning through her, it urged her to press down, ignoring the jolt of pain before she started to writhe against him. Within two or three thrusts, it no longer hurt, and then it started to feel amazing.

His hips were jutting upward now too, taking her as rapidly as she was taking him. Daisy threw back her head, her curls falling down her back, so he bent forward to lift one of her breasts, taking it into his mouth and sucking on her nipple firmly. She'd never been with a man before, especially not during estrus, so she'd been unprepared for the intensity of the emotions it evoked.

It wasn't just a physical feeling of well-being and pleasure. There was an emotional element to this she had never expected. She felt cherished and cosseted, even as he thrusted into her with a violent intensity that she was matching, needing to come to alleviate the ache inside.

He reached between them to stroke her clit. Daisy cried out, opening her mouth in a shout of euphoria as her orgasm started to crash over her. He continued to thrust, maintaining the rapid tempo and his hardness as he coaxed another orgasm from her. It was only as she started to slowly relax from that one that his cock inside her twitched, and spasms of his release filled her.

She keened with pleasure at the sensation, which brought her another climax, and her sheath tightened around him when his cock swelled, the base knotting to keep them together. He was breeding her, and in her primitive mindset at the moment, that was all she wanted in the world.

His mouth went to her scent gland again, licking frantically. When his teeth scraped against her, she moaned. Part of her wanted to press against him, urging him to claim her, but a stronger part of her warned her to pull away. She couldn't move at all, and the decision was left to him. She didn't know if she was relieved or upset when he pulled away without biting her.

It took some time for the animalistic haze to fade and for normal, rational thought to return. As the fever abated, Daisy realized she was still joined with a complete stranger, lying on his lap with his shaft buried inside her, knotted to keep them together. Her eyes widened with alarm, and she sat up quickly, making him wince at the way it tugged on his cock inside her. Fear filled her, and she was frantic to escape.

"Easy, Daisy." His tone was soothing, and so were his hands as they clasped her shoulders, squeezing gently. "I won't hurt you."

She hated how she was driven to respond to that note of tender authority, which rendered her muscles looser and took some of her fear. She stared at him uncertainly. "I don't even know your name." She had shared such a frantic, frenzied mating with an Alpha whose name she didn't even know. Even now, his sperm would be trying to meet her egg and produce new life with a man who was a stranger. She dropped her head in shame at her own behavior, tears burning her eyes.

Gently, he nudged up her chin with his fingers, forcing her to look at him. "I'm Ryder Strang, and I want you to know I never would've bought an Omega under normal circumstances. You were just so frantic with need, and I couldn't resist the impulse to take care of you. That's my biological imperative."

She shook her head. "Alphas are dangerous, abusive, and selfish. You don't own me. Just because you paid some alien who kidnapped me doesn't mean you own me."

He surprised her by nodding. "I agree. As I said, I was responding to the need to help you."

She glared at him, squirming on his lap as his knot started to soften. "You were clearly helping yourself as well, Alpha."

His eyes narrowed. "If you recall, I offered you the option of staying in the box and filtering out your pheromones to prevent me going into rut. I was prepared to find you suppressant, but you begged for me. It's like catnip to an Alpha. I could no more resist your needs than I can suppress the urge to take care of you. That's how I'm wired."

She was still angry at his actions, but she was forced to reevaluate her opinion as she recalled him making the offer. She'd been disoriented with fever and need, so she hadn't been able to seriously entertain the idea. Even now, she couldn't imagine she could have lasted another hour, at minimum, while he tried to find suppressant for her, and she nodded grudgingly. "I concede we were both forced to act because of our biology. That's over now."

"Nearly." He looked down wryly, where their bodies were joined. "I should be able to release you in a few minutes." His eyes closed for a moment, and he looked utterly sated. "I had no idea it would be like this with an Omega."

In spite of herself, she was intrigued by the awe in his tone. "You've never taken an Omega before?"

His eyes opened, and he shook his head. "I've only ever met a few. The last one I met was at a market planet a few weeks ago, and she was mated to her Alpha, Remy. Maya was her name, but I felt no attraction, because she was already claimed. I've only ever been with Beta women, and one Alpha female." He closed his eyes and grimaced, clearly recalling that incident with a hint of reluctance.

"I didn't expect it to be like this either." She gave the admission grudgingly, relieved when he softened enough she could pull away from him and stand up. Immediately aware of her nudity, she searched around for the jumpsuit she'd worn, finding it crumpled in the box. She rushed over and donned it. By the time she turned back to him, fully dressed, he was also wearing his flight suit and was in the process of strapping on his armor again.

He seemed like a decent enough guy, especially for an Alpha. She cleared her throat as she moved closer. "I need your help."

His eyes widened, and they also darkened slightly. The hazel was ringed with silver from his rut, and she knew her eyes were probably the same and would be for a while until all vestiges of her estrus faded.

"What do you need?"

"I need to return to that ship and rescue the other Omega, Azaria. She's more like my sister than a friend. Please, Alpha." It was instinct to call him that, along with the tone she used.

She could tell from his body language he wasn't going to agree even before he shook his head. "It wouldn't be safe. How could the two of us hope to rescue her? She's probably been sold by now anyway."

Daisy crossed her arms over her chest, trying to push back the wave of tiredness sweeping over her. Ryder seem to be suffering similarly, so she assumed it was a natural consequence of their frantic mating. "She's like a sister to me. I can't just leave her to her fate."

"I get it." He sighed as he stood up, coming to stand near her. He seemed like he might reach for her, but apparently decided she wasn't in the frame of mind to accept his touch readily. His hand remained firmly at his side. "I have a brother, so I understand how you feel, but I don't see how we can do anything about it."

She glared at him. "You don't have to do anything besides return me. I'll find her myself."

He let out a scoffing sound. "Or the Klinoks will find you first, shoot you full of more enhancer, and sell you all over again. Is that what you want?"

With an angry sigh, she shook her head and looked away from him. He had a valid point. She really didn't want to be sold to a different Alpha. She wasn't all that happy to have been sold to this one, but at least he didn't seem to be as bad as the Alphas she'd heard about while living at the convent.

He was the first one she'd ever met, since the sisters cloistered themselves on the planet to avoid interacting with Alphas, but just because this one appeared to be kind didn't mean Mother Risa was inaccurate in her information about Alphas typically being self-absorbed, selfish, and unmoved by the pain they might cause Omegas.

"I don't want to be captured again."

He stifled a yawn. "In that case, I suggest we lie down. It's a natural reaction following estrus and rutting. We'll probably both sleep for hours."

Reluctantly, she followed him from the bridge after he secured it using his A.I. program, set on autopilot. She eagerly watched the code he inputted to do so, though she tried to appear like she wasn't. He didn't seem to realize there was anything off about her interest, and he led her down the hallway to the sole quarters a moment later.

She was nervous as she stepped inside with him, thinking he expected her to sleep with him, and perhaps more, so it was a pleasant surprise when he gestured to a loveseat. "I'll take that, and you can have the bed."

"No, that's okay." She preferred to be closer to the door. "I'm much shorter than you are, and I don't see how you can fold yourself onto that, Mr. Strang."

He gave her a strange smile. "I think you can call me Ryder. We're that familiar, aren't we?" His hazel eyes twinkled with amusement that was difficult to ignore.

She allowed herself a small smile. "Yes, I suppose we are."

He looked at the loveseat and then the bed for a moment. "I suppose I should argue about this and insist you take the bed, but the truth is, neither one is particularly comfortable. I've been saving up money for more important things, like keeping the ship running." He winced then.

She frowned at him. "What's wrong?"

His neck turned red, and he shrugged. "Nothing. Nothing important."

As he moved to the bed, she heard him mutter something about rathium bars, but she couldn't quite make it out.

She was genuinely feeling exhaustion creeping over her as well, so she did her best to curl up in an uncomfortable position on the loveseat. The lumpy furniture made it difficult to relax, and she was relieved it would be harder to fall asleep. She kept her eyes mostly closed as she watched him settle into bed. He stripped off his armor but left on the flight suit, and she appreciated that, though part of her mourned not getting another glimpse of his gorgeous Alpha body.

She'd hardly had a chance to appreciate the male beauty of it earlier, caught in the throes of estrus. Now, she allowed herself to remember what she could of that overwhelming, frantic coupling, deciding he must have quite a beautiful body. It was enough to cause a stirring of arousal again, but she quickly forced her thoughts elsewhere. She didn't want to risk entering another cycle of estrus, or she might never be able to catch up with Azaria.

He was asleep a short time later, confirmed by gentle snoring. She waited a few minutes longer, pinching her arm a few times to keep from falling asleep, before quietly easing off the loveseat and approaching his door. He hadn't bothered to lock it, so all she had to do was press the button instead of applying her palm, and it opened with a hydraulic hiss.

She watched him carefully to make sure he didn't wake up, but he only stirred slightly before turning more onto his left side. Once she was sure he wasn't going to wake, she tiptoed through the door, closing it behind her. Then she moved down the hallway and retraced their steps back to the command deck. Fortunately, it was a small freighter, so it made it easy to navigate.

When she reached the command deck, she unlocked the ship using the code he'd inputted. She didn't know a lot about technology, but she thought his system might be outdated, since it didn't require a biometric scan to unlock. Maybe that function didn't work. Whatever the case, she was relieved the code brought up the navigation system. "Computer, locate the Klinok market ship and plan a course."

Lights on the console flashed for a moment, and the computer's male voice, with a rich timber and faint accent she didn't recognize, said, "Coordinates confirmed."

"Lock in and proceed." She hoped that was the right terminology, since she hadn't spent much time flying. She'd taken out a skid a few times on the planet to run errands to the nearby moon, where the sisters sometimes traded with the farmers (all Betas) who lived there, but that was the extent of her traveling aside from the Klinoks kidnapping her and bringing her this far.

She tried to stay awake, but exhaustion was creeping over her. It was a long stretch of time to have nothing to do when she was so exhausted, and the third time her head slumped forward to rest on her chest, Daisy wasn't able to make herself rouse enough to lift it and try to stay awake. Instead, she dozed off.

"WHAT ARE YOU DOING?"

Daisy roused abruptly at the angry tone of the Alpha towering over her. Part of her trembled, and it took everything she had not to submit with a squeak and beg his forgiveness. She ruthlessly squashed the urge and stared up at him, trying to appear unafraid and unaffected. "I'm looking for the Klinok ship so I can find Azaria."

He scowled at her. "Did you wait until I'd fallen asleep to sneak out?"

She shrugged a shoulder. "What if I did? You weren't going to help me." She was afraid he might snatch the opportunity away from her now, though when she looked at the nav system, they were about to catch up with the Klinok ship.

He growled at her, and the sound made her tremble with a little bit of fear, but oddly, a strong sense of anticipation. She had to quell the reaction.

"I should turn the ship around right now."

She waved at the console. "I guess I can't stop you."

He glared at her. "I don't like being forced into situations, Omega," he said with a strong hint of reprimand.

Most likely, if she had been his mated Omega, she would've been unable to hold out against him being displeased with her. The way she'd heard it from the sisters, she would practically be his trained dog if she submitted as an Omega was wired to do. Abruptly, she remembered he'd never bitten her to formalize any claim, and she was strictly relieved about that. Of course, she was. "I don't like being denied a chance to save my friend."

With a scowl, he moved to a different seat. She expected him to reprogram the coordinates, but instead, he simply stared at them for a moment. "Fine. We're almost there, so I'll take my skid over and see if I can find out any information about who bought her. You have to accept she's probably long gone by now, but maybe we can find a way to track her down. Will that satisfy you?"

Her chest felt like it fizzed with bubbles of happiness, and she smiled at him. It was a warm, genuine smile, and when he purred softly, she felt like preening around the command deck. She forced herself to stay seated. "Thank you, Ryder." It was a struggle not to call him Alpha. And she hated that impulse.

He departed the ship as soon as they were in skid range. She hadn't asked to go with him, realizing her scent and unclaimed status would still put her at risk of being discovered or taken by any other Alphas who might remain aboard the Klinok ship. Instead, she paced restlessly around the command room, hoping Ryder could find out something about Azaria's fate, something actionable they could use to save her friend.

As she paced, her mind kept returning to the penultimate moment of their mating, just before he came inside her. It should've been the natural point where he bit her, claiming her as his Omega.

Why was she so upset he had quelled the urge to do so? She didn't know a thing about him, and though he might be a decent Alpha, he could also be a horrible, abusive one. She should be thanking her lucky stars he had no intention of claiming her rather than feeling incensed he chose not to. Why would she want to be permanently bound to an Alpha she didn't even know anyway?

Telling herself she was being ridiculous and irrational, she tried to talk herself out of caring that he hadn't claimed her. The only benefit would have come from the protection his claim would afford her from other Alphas until she could return home to Paladin.

Once she was home, it wouldn't matter anyway, though she intended to make sure she joined the rank of the sisters who protected them all. It was high time she learned how to fight and defend not just herself, but the other sisters at the Omega convent. If she had before, perhaps she could have helped stem the tide rather than end up being the first one abducted.

A pang of guilt shot through her when she recalled Azaria had been trying to rescue her, which was how her friend had been taken as well. Unlike Azaria, Daisy was relatively useless when it came to self-defense, and she no longer found that acceptable. She also couldn't stand the fact that her inability to take care of herself had led to Azaria's kidnapping and being sold to someone else, and she owed it to her friend to save her if they could.

Chapter Four

RYDER PASSED THROUGH the airlock of his ship a while later, finding himself even more credits lighter, though he still had enough to maintain expenses for a couple of months. He'd acquired the information he needed from the auctioneer's bursar, who seemed to think he was wanting to pillage someone else's Omega to keep a harem. The bursar hadn't cared his reason for wanting to know who bought the other female. He'd been content with counting the credits he'd accepted in exchange for the frequency of the ship's beacon and speculated final destination.

He had barely exited the cargo hold when she came to meet him, her gaze expectant. It disconcerted him how much he wanted to please her, to wipe away the anxiety from her expression and have it replaced with joy instead. He stiffened his resolve, pushing aside his Alpha impulses to take care of her, and did his best to keep his expression neutral. He didn't want to reveal too much yet, since the news was a mix of good and bad.

She was practically hopping in place. "Well?"

"Your friend was purchased by a known criminal mastermind with his own little empire. Have you heard of Aldrich Garros?"

She blinked, but didn't show a flicker of recognition. "I haven't."

He frowned. "You must not spend much time in this sector of the galaxy then. He's notorious."

She hesitated for a moment before saying, "Aside from this misadventure, I've never really left Paladin once I was taken there."

He frowned, searching his memory for any mention of the planet name. "I don't believe I've heard of that planet. Where is it?"

Her silence spoke volumes, indicating she had no plans to tell him. Instead, she said, "There's a convent for Omegas there. We can take refuge from your kind."

He frowned. "You've grown up in a convent?" He couldn't help his scowl of disapproval while imagining what kind of nonsense had been stuffed into her head by a bunch of matronly Omegas who were too afraid of Alphas to live among them. It was true there were too many selfish Alphas, but there were just as many good ones, or at least he liked to think so, who responded to their biological imperative to protect and safeguard their Omegas and anyone else weaker than them. "That explains a lot."

She frowned at him but didn't pursue the topic of conversation. Instead she said, "You know how to find her." She spoke it as a statement of fact.

His poker face must've revealed more than he planned. With a small sigh, he nodded once. "I do, but I don't think it's a good idea. These guys will be heavily armed, and if we can't intercept the ship before it reaches his planet, we have no chance of getting her out."

Her rigid posture and stiff expression indicated she wasn't going to be open to logic, at least not when it came to this. "I'm going with or without you. I'll find a way if you'll just drop me at the next planet."

He didn't bother to remind her what kind of risk she would take as an unmated Omega. Instead, he said, "I didn't tell you I wouldn't help you. I'm just telling you the odds are significantly against us." His breath caught in his throat, and he grinned at her. "I might have a way to even them though. If Quinn is close..." He trailed off as he moved to the lift to go to the command deck, entering the command room a few minutes later.

"Who's Quinn?" she asked, following right behind him.

"My brother. I believe I mentioned him earlier. If he's in the area, I know he'll help us." He could also help Azaria if they actually managed to rescue her. He doubted she had been compromised already, since she was likely purchased strictly for Aldrich's pleasure, and he suspected none of his men, even Alphas among them, would have wanted to risk the gangster's fury at stealing his prize.

When they rescued her, she was going to be in a similar state, if not worse, than Daisy had been, and he couldn't even recall what her friend looked like. He'd had eyes only for Daisy, and if he'd seen Azaria at all, it hadn't registered. The idea of satisfying her need felt repulsive to him, unlike the pull he'd had the moment he saw Daisy.

"You should call him then."

He stifled a grin as he turned away from her, deciding she was a bossy little thing for an Omega. He quite liked that about her. So far, there wasn't much he didn't like about her. Even her obstinate streak had its charms, despite the fact it was placing them in danger.

He soon hailed Quinn's ship, the computer bringing up an image of his brother on the screen. He heard her gasp and realized she must've seen the resemblance between them. Quinn was two years older, and he had harder features and looked a little more like their father while he resembled their mother.

Despite different shades of eyes, they had the same shade of hair. Where Ryder wore his short, Quinn allowed it to grow long and free, falling down his back. He looked like a barbarian warrior even in his flight suit, and his beard was shaggier than the last time he'd seen his brother a few weeks before.

"What's up, Spud?"

He flushed as she giggled at the nickname. "I've told you not to call me that."

"Of course, Spud," said his brother with a wicked gleam in his eye. She giggled again, and his expression changed. "Is that a feminine laugh I hear?" His brother seemed intrigued.

His hackles rose, and he couldn't resist the urge to growl at his brother.

"Easy." Quinn's eyes widened, and it was obvious he was reading more into the reaction than he should have. "Have you claimed an Omega?"

"No," said Ryder roughly. "I have taken one aboard to help her though. I need your help as well. We're trying to rescue her friend, who was sold by the Klinoks."

Quinn frowned. "You want to go up against the Klinoks? They have a huge fleet, and even the Coalition enforcers avoid them whenever possible." His brother's shoulder stiffened. "Of course, if you're in, I'm in."

Ryder shook his head. "She's already been sold, though it's almost as bad. Aldrich Garros is her new owner."

Quinn's eyes widened, and he shook his head. "You can't think to invade Garros's planet? There's just the two of us and our two ships. It'll never happen, Spud."

This time, Daisy didn't giggle at the nickname. Instead, she surged forward to confront his brother, shoving him out of the way. "She hasn't been taken there yet. She's still *en route*, which means it's just one ship. Ryder has already agreed to help me. Will you please do the same? Azaria needs to be rescued before it's too late."

His brother hesitated for only a moment before nodding. "I'll help you however I can, miss. Are you there, Ryder?"

Ryder gently moved her aside again so he could step in front of the camera. "I'm here. Where are you?"

"I'm sending you my coordinates now. I suggest we meet up about halfway. That should be roughly close to the planet."

"I think so. We just want to make sure we get to them before they get to Garros."

"Agreed."

After his brother had signed off, Daisy turned to him. "Thank you for helping me, and for getting him to help us too."

He shrugged a shoulder as he eased back into his chair. "If things go well, he can serve more than one function today. Your friend's likely to be in a similar state to what you were earlier. Unless she can ride it out until she can get a suppressant, she'll need an Alpha to help her."

Daisy's expression turned cold. "I'm surprised you don't plan to be that Alpha. You could get lucky twice in one day."

He scowled up at her, clenching his hands around the armrests to keep from surging to his feet. "I think you've underestimated me, Omega." He used the word deliberately, watching her shudder with a combination of pleasure and irritation, likely at her response to the word. "I have no wish to claim any Omega, and certainly not a second one today."

For a second, her expression was full of wounded pain, but it was gone a moment later as she blinked and nodded at him just once. Her gaze drifted over his shoulder, carefully averted from his. "It still surprises me. Alphas take what they want or can get."

"Some Alphas take whatever they want, but I'm not among them." He spoke the words firmly as he turned away from her. "Why don't you try to get some more rest?"

With a sniff in his direction, she turned and exited the command room. He waited a few minutes to ensure she wasn't going to return before he called Quinn once again.

"What's the plan, Spud?"

He gritted his teeth at the nickname, but he ignored it. "I don't really have one yet, other than intercepting the ship, getting it to stop somehow, and freeing Azaria. You need to know she'll be in estrus." He quickly explained how Daisy had crossed his path.

His brother shook his head. "You spent a whole year's worth of credits to buy an Omega? That isn't like you at all."

Ryder flushed. "I realize that, but she was in such clear pain that I couldn't deny the need to help her. You know how it is as an Alpha."

His brother snorted. "I try not to be that Alpha."

He held his tongue, knowing Quinn had good reason for rejecting his role as Alpha, which made it more difficult to broach the subject he'd called about. "About Azaria… If she doesn't have the fortitude to wait 'til we can find a suppressant, will you be able to help her?"

Quinn frowned. "Why can't you? You didn't claim Daisy."

He flushed again. "I can't explain it, but the idea of being with another Omega makes me physically ill."

Quinn's eyes widened for a moment, the dark-brown depths filled with a gleam of interest. "I see. I'm sure you've heard the fairytale that every Alpha has an ideal Omega, one who is perfect for him and vice versa?"

Ryder shrugged. "Who hasn't heard that nonsense?" He was pleased by the conviction in his tone, which hid the fact that once upon a time as a younger man, he'd actually bought into it. He'd spent a while looking for his Omega only to never find one at all who wasn't already attached to someone else. He'd seen more than one Omega trapped in a relationship with an Alpha who mistreated her, but it had been out of his power to help her in any fashion. Once the bond was sealed, it was only breakable by death. Even then, some Alphas clung to the bond with their deceased Omegas.

"Just be careful of your heart. The last thing you want to do is claim an Omega and be responsible for her." Quinn swiped his hand down his face. "I can't promise anything, but maybe I can try to help her. If not, we can always sedate her until we can find some suppressant."

"You have sedative on your ship, 'cause I'm out?" It had been a lean few months for him, especially as Garros started to take over the sector. He refused to work for a criminal like that, not wanting to owe anyone that kind of loyalty or be involved that deeply in illegal activities. A scarcity of jobs had left his medical supplies dwindled down to nothing as well as a lot of his other things, including fuel and maintenance. Even food was getting critically low. He was glad to have some of the rathium credits remaining, and despite the dire circumstances, he couldn't regret having spent the rest to rescue Daisy.

"I do. I had a successful salvage operation recently. Do you need to borrow some money?"

Ryder frowned. "No, I'll find a way to make it work." He assumed there would be another opportunity to smuggle more of the rathium bars. Just because he'd indicated he was out of the operation didn't mean he couldn't get back in if needed. They were always looking for people willing to do it, since the prison sentence was stiff if one was caught with rathium. The Coalition considered it a vital fuel source, so it ran the whole empire, and they didn't take kindly to their reserves being appropriated and redistributed.

"I'm not promising, but I'll help her if I can."

Ryder nodded, knowing he'd have to accept that. Quinn had justification for feeling the way he did, and Ryder hated to ask him, but he also didn't think he could be the one to help this Azaria through her estrus.

Perhaps the physical imperative would take over, as it was designed to, and he'd be able to get past his squeamish disgust at the idea, but it would haunt him if he did so. He was convinced touching her friend would be a betrayal to Daisy despite their lack of formal bonding.

Chapter Five

DAISY RETURNED TO THE command deck when the computer signaled to her they were close to intercepting the *Stargazer*. She eyed the ship they were planning to attack with a little trepidation as the *Remedy's* computer offered a schematic. It was at least three times the size of the two ships put together, and they had more firepower. What they didn't have was Quinn's stealth system and Ryder's flair for strategy.

She listened to the two brothers bicker quietly, but without heat, as they discussed the best way to intercept the ship. Finally, they both agreed they would take out the engine first by combining their firepower, then they would focus on the gun turrets. Their last target would be the artificial gravity system. Once they removed that, it would leave the people on the ship in disarray, and they'd be struggling to maintain their balance and not get disoriented when they boarded.

She realized Ryder was moving his seat from facing his brother to the controls. He was apparently planning to manually target. She might've questioned the hubris of another, but he had such confident command she had no doubt he would be just as competent, if not more so, than the A.I. system that helped run the ship.

She held her breath when he and Quinn got into position, coordinating together. Moments later, she held her breath again as Ryder pressed the firing mechanism to open fire on the ship ahead of them. Quinn's fire was visible from his ship through the starboard window, and she moved over to the other side so she could see the ship itself.

The *Stargazer* immediately dropped out of ionospace, so their targeting had been true. It stuttered along for a bit, trying to return fire, but Ryder shifted his attention to the gun turrets, taking them out before they became much of a threat either.

She looked over at the starboard window again in time to see Quinn's ship changing its targeting, to what she assumed was the gravitational mechanism. When his face appeared on the screen a second after that, he was beaming. "All three systems are down."

"Let's get aboard and get her friend as quickly as possible."

"I'll meet you there."

Ryder stood up and rushed from the command room. Daisy's legs were shorter, so she had to run to keep up, but she arrived at the cargo bay with him. As she reached for his spare E-suit, he growled at her and took it out of her hand. She glared at him. "What are you doing? I can't go without that."

He scowled as he placed it back on the hook. "You're not going at all. You're staying here."

She put her hands on her hips. "Azaria will try to fight you if I'm not with you. You'll lose precious time, and you might have to hurt her to get her to come with you. Everyone's going to be disoriented, and I need to be there to reassure her."

He scowled again. "It isn't safe. I won't risk you."

There was a fluttering sensation in her chest at his words, and he seemed so determined to protect her, but she was able to stifle the instinctive response with the reminder that was his biological imperative. It didn't mean he actually felt protective of her or worried about her personally. She swallowed down the lump in her throat and faced him. "I'm coming along. It doesn't matter if it's dangerous."

His eyes widened. "Are you mad? Of course it matters."

She allowed a soft smile and fluttered her lashes a little. "It doesn't matter, because I know you'll keep me safe. You're an Alpha, and that's your job."

He growled at her, and he looked displeased, but she knew she had him. He couldn't ignore his nature, and though he might be angry at her for using that against him, he must have decided there was little point in arguing. With a grunt, he lifted the suit and passed it to her again. "Hurry up. Quinn's no doubt waiting for us already."

She glared at him as she started to wiggle into the suit. "I'm not the one who wasted time arguing."

He heaved a sigh that sounded like he was being burdened with all the weight in the galaxy before turning away from her. When he turned back, he handed her a laser pistol. "It's not much, but it should last you for about ten minutes or a hundred shots. It's old, and the charging mechanism doesn't work as well as it should, so keep that in mind. Unless you're in an active firing situation, keep it flipped off to maintain power for as long as possible."

She nodded as she slipped it into the holster built into the E-suit and followed him to his skid. She stood with him on it, pressing against him in her fear, though she hated revealing the weakness. She'd never been fond of flying, especially on a skid with nothing enclosing her, and though the E-suit had the ability to lock in with magnets that would keep her from being thrown off, she was still nervous.

As though he sensed that, and he probably did with his Alpha instincts, he put his arm around her waist and held her against him while the airlock opened, and they entered space. He directed the skid toward the ship that was currently floating, and she saw Quinn already had a head start. He was much closer than they were, but he was clearly waiting for them.

He lifted his wrist and tapped it in an impatient motion as they reached him. "It took you long enough, Spud," he said through the speaker in her suit. She giggled again, wondering how in the world a virile Alpha like Ryder had ended up with the nickname Spud. It was a story she would have to remember to ask for later, since now wasn't the time.

"We had a little delay." He sent her a look that clearly placed all the blame on her. She wrinkled her nose and looked away from him.

Quinn sounded surprised and looked that way to see her. "You let your Omega come along?"

"She's not my Omega."

Daisy stiffened at the words, hating how much they injured her pride. It was strictly her pride, of course. She sniffed at him again before addressing Quinn. "Azaria won't know you, and she'll fight. I didn't want to delay her rescue."

"It's my understanding she's locked in a box. How could she fight?"

She scowled at his dispassionate response. "Maybe she couldn't fight, but she'd get worked up and scared for no reason. If she sees me, she'll be a lot more relaxed, okay?" She couldn't help her hint of impatience at his lack of empathy.

He shrugged a shoulder. "Let's get this over with."

Using his wrist comm, Quinn forced the door open, and they entered the cargo hold a moment later. She quickly disengaged the mag lock of her E-suit and hopped off the skid a second after Ryder. He held a hand to help her, but she was already down, so she ignored it. He dropped it to his side a second later, and the three of them exited the cargo hold.

When they entered the corridor, they found three large Alphas waiting for them, and Daisy had already drawn her gun. So had the two Alphas with her, and they made short work of the three of them. Her shots went wild, and she looked at Ryder as they moved down the corridor once it was clear. "Is the calibration off on this thing?"

He shrugged a shoulder. "It could be. It's only ever been a spare, and it hasn't been serviced for a while."

For the first time, Daisy realized when he bought her, he had probably put himself in a tight situation. She supposed she should be more grateful than resentful as she had been, though she couldn't help feeling hurt he had bought her long enough to fuck her but had no interest in keeping her.

It was a crazy thought, since she didn't want to be kept by him anyway. She sighed with impatience at herself as she followed behind the two of them, since they made her stay behind them.

She heard a scuffling sound behind her and turned just as a large Alpha, even bigger than Quinn, who was the largest Alpha she'd ever seen, darted out from a bend in the corridor and shoved her to the ground. His weight was on her, and she grimaced at the way his hard cock pressed into the cleft of her buttocks. She had no doubt this Alpha would claim her if he got the chance.

Only the E-suit blocking her pheromones was probably keeping him from rutting. She prayed she would be able to stave off going into estrus again. She didn't know if the enhancer was still in her system. If not, she should have finished with estrus for at least the next month, but she wasn't certain she had.

Fortunately, all his rubbing against her did was make her queasy, and he was soon off her. She heard a ferocious growl and looked up in time to see Ryder lifting the Alpha, who was quite a bit larger than him, and throwing him across the corridor. The man slammed into the wall, groaned, and crumpled to the floor a moment later. He laid at an unnatural angle that suggested he wouldn't be getting up again.

She looked up at him, and the ferocious possessiveness in his gaze made her heart skip a beat, and slick started to flood her. She was thankful the E-suit filtered out her pheromones so he wouldn't respond. The last thing they needed was to get caught in the throes of estrus and rutting while they were trying to rescue Azaria.

She looked away from him, using every ounce of strength she had, and somehow managed to regain control of her body. The slick was still there, proof of how much she wanted him, but at least it was no longer dripping copiously from her, and she wasn't at risk of being lost in the thrall of estrus now.

The three of them proceeded onward, using coordinates Quinn must have programed into his wrist comm provided by Ryder to identify her friend's biomarkers. They seemed to know where they were going, and they reached the area a short time later. The guards here hadn't yet had a chance to put on antigravity boots, so they were still floating around and clinging to the wall.

She found it an amusing sight, and she was further amused when Ryder reached up and took the gun from one of the guards before shoving him across the room. He went flying, colliding with the window, which he clung to in a desperate bid to keep himself semi-upright.

Quinn dealt with the other with a swift punch that sent him to the ceiling, where he hovered, clearly knocked out.

Quinn's wrist comm eased the way for them once more, hacking through the code that kept them barred from the room inside. The hydraulic hiss of the door opening an instant later echoed through her suit, and she saw Azaria's box from the corner of her eye. She tried to rush in, but Ryder held her back, insisting on going first. She rolled her eyes, but she understood that was his nature, so she impatiently followed right behind him, with Quinn bringing up the rear.

Azaria was in a sorry state, and Daisy winced on her friend's behalf. She remembered how frantic she had been just a few hours ago, and it had been that much longer for poor Azaria. She was probably burning up with fever, and she might even have some permanent damage from how long she'd been kept in estrus.

Ryder was looking at his brother with care and concern. "Can you help her?"

She watched his brother approach the box slowly, his posture stiff with reluctance. Yet he knelt before her, putting a hand against the clear wall of the box as she did the same. Azaria was whimpering, the sound audible through the suit, and she pleaded with both her eyes and her words when Quinn was before her.

"Alpha, make it stop hurting." Her black eyes were luminous with unshed tears, and her face was red with exertion of the fever. Her dark brown hair was plastered to her face and hanging down around it in limp strands coated with sweat. She was clearly suffering.

"I'll help her." With those words, Quinn lifted her box, clearly disdaining Ryder's offer to help. "I've got her, but you need to make sure the path stays clear. Same for you, Daisy." He sounded gruff, and there was definitely a hint of growl in his tone.

He hadn't even smelled her friend's pheromones yet, and he was already responding. She wondered if this was how it had been for Ryder, and she had a new appreciation for the compulsion to buy her that had gripped him. How had he managed to offer her the choice of a suppressant before just taking her if his need had been as urgent as Quinn's?

That worried her, and she stepped in front of Quinn. He looked down at her with surprise, and he seemed to be straining, though she doubted it was under the weight of the box housing her friend and Azaria's weight itself. "Move."

She put her hands on her hips, somehow managing to stand up to the note of authority in his tone. Maybe because he wasn't her Alpha—not that she had an Alpha, she hastily assured herself. "You have to give her a choice. Ryder gave me a choice, and you have to do the same for Azaria."

He hesitated for a moment before nodding once. "I plan to. I don't have suppressant, but I have sedatives if she wants to wait until we can get suppressant. I'll take her aboard my ship in case she chooses the other option. If not, I'll send her to you as soon as it's safe."

She frowned as she moved aside, knowing she had to accept his word. She had no reason to trust him, but she found herself doing so anyway. There was a forthrightness about the gruff Quinn that made her think he wasn't one for lying or dishonesty. If he planned to take her friend without waiting for her consent, she was sure he would've just told her that bluntly, reminding her he was an Alpha, and his word was law above an Omega's.

She stepped back, brushing against Ryder, who squeezed her hand in a reassuring fashion before they departed the quarters. They ran into one more set of guards, composed of Beta males, and the brothers made quick work of them. Daisy managed to figure out how to use the laser pistol and compensate for its uncalibrated sights and took out one herself before they reached the cargo hold.

Quinn stepped onto his skid, setting down the box with Azaria in it. Daisy tried to catch her friend's glance, but Azaria was staring at Quinn with open need and naked desire, having eyes for no one else. Quinn seemed to be in a similar state, so she gave up any attempt to communicate with her friend, at least until the frenetic madness of estrus had eased.

Instead, she tried to trust in her own instincts that told her Quinn wouldn't hurt her friend, and he had been kind enough to help Ryder rescue her, so she joined Ryder on his skid, locked in the mag lock, and clung to him once more as the airlock opened, and the two skids went their separate ways to their respective ships.

They were back on the *Remedy* a short time later, and she removed the E-suit and passed it to him after he hung his as well. She paced a little bit.

"What's wrong?"

She stopped and looked at him. "I guess I'm just impatient to know what's happening. We can't leave until she makes a decision, because if she wants to go back with me to the convent, we have to take her with us."

He frowned. "You want to go to the convent?"

She nodded. "It's my home. I have no reason to stay." As she said the words, she uttered them with an air of challenge, realizing she was asking him to give her a reason to change her mind, a reason to stay with him.

Chapter Six

RYDER LOOKED AT HER, shocked that she would be ready to walk away from him. He shouldn't feel so desperate to keep her, since they weren't bonded, and all they had done was mate during her estrus. That shouldn't have been enough to bind them together, or to make him have a stake in her future, but the idea of her leaving him was more than he could stand. With a growl, he surged forward and pulled her into his arms. "You aren't going anywhere. Your place is with me."

She stared up at him, slowly licking her lips. "I don't feel like that's the case. You have no interest in claiming me, Ryder, and you certainly can't keep me this way. I'm better off at the convent."

"You're better off with me." With another growl, he bent his head and kissed her firmly. He expected some resistance, since she seemed angry with him, or at least challenging his right to claim her, but instead, she melted right into his arms.

The kiss was hard and hungry, but he tried to gentle it when some shredds of his control returned, dragging her closer as he inhaled her scent. He moved his mouth from hers to her neck, sniffing and licking her scent gland. It caused her pheromones to rise, and he could smell the slick on her.

At first, it was an older scent, but then it was fresh and prodigious, and he knew she was actively producing it right then. She wanted him as much as he wanted her. He was determined to do it right this time, so instead of giving in to the impulse to pin her to the wall and take her right there in the cargo bay, he lifted her into his arms. She let out a squeal as she clung to him, and he hurried down the corridor into the lift.

He put her down long enough to nuzzle her neck again while they waited for the lift to take them to the deck with his bedroom, and then he picked her up once more. This time, her thighs wrapped around his waist as she faced him while he carried her, his hands supporting the rounded globes of her ass that he squeezed with delight.

He was thankful the biometric panel on his door was broken, so all he had to do was nudge it with his elbow and not let go of her to open the door and take her inside. Once he was in his room, he lowered her to her feet, his hands going to the fasteners of her suit to rip it open. She moaned her pleasure as he stripped it from her, revealing her ebony skin and utter perfection. He hadn't had as much time to appreciate it earlier in the throes of rut, but now, he could take his time to savor each part of her.

Ryder let his hands roam over her smooth skin and soft curves, growling with impatience when she blocked him. He soon realized she just wanted him to remove his armor and flight suit, so he stepped back to accommodate her.

He planned to pick her up and sweep her to bed, but she dropped to her knees before him. He put a hand in her hair, wrapping the springy curls around his fist. "You don't have to..." He trailed off with a groan as her hand wrapped around his large cock, her fingers not quite touching. She stroked him tentatively at first, but as his arousal grew, her enthusiasm seemed to increase, and she was soon jerking harder on his shaft while bringing her mouth forward to taste a drop of pre-cum that glistened on the tip.

Ryder nearly lost all control when her shy little tongue stroked against him in such a sensitive place. He couldn't last if she continued to do that. With a groan, he pushed her away, but carefully, before bending to lift and carry her to the bed. He dropped her on it unceremoniously as he followed her down.

His mouth sought out hers, and she moaned and writhed underneath him when his tongue slipped into her mouth. He wanted to be gentle and take his time, now that they were no longer locked in the throes of biological imperative, but he still needed her with a frantic edge that had him practically devouring her as his mouth took control.

She wasn't having trouble keeping up though. Her tongue plunged into his mouth to taste him as her hands gripped his shoulders tightly enough for him to feel her nails digging into his skin. Those pinpricks of pain helped him regain some semblance of control and keep from thrusting into her.

With a low groan of reluctance, he tore his mouth from hers, gliding it down her neck. He paused to nibble the column of her throat, making her purr. The sound caused a corresponding rumble in his chest, and he wasn't sure if he felt contentment or ecstasy right then.

A couple of deep breaths helped him focus, and he moved his mouth lower. He detoured to sample one plump nipple, the brown bud tempting him to take it and part of her areola inside to suck firmly. That made her hips bump upward, reminding him what delights awaited, which helped him release her nipple and continue his journey south.

When he reached her core a few seconds later, she trembled as he breathed against her. "Ryder." She sounded uncertain.

He lifted his head to make sure she was looking at him. "It's okay. I won't hurt you."

She whimpered before he lowered his head again, kissing the lips of her mound before allowing his tongue to trace the neatly trimmed line of hair he found there. Her musk coated his tongue as she produced more slick before he even dipped inside.

Daisy shouted when he touched her swollen clit with the tip of his tongue. Her lower body came off the bed, and he gently applied pressure to her thighs to keep her from squirming away. He used a light, deft touch to stroke and taste her, surrounded by her scent and unique flavor. It was almost enough to make him come right then.

She was thrashing against him now, clearly chasing her release, and he didn't want to torture her. He dipped his tongue farther down, licking her slit until he reached her opening. When his tongue wriggled inside,

Daisy sobbed, and her hands clenched in his hair. He winced at the force she applied as she pulled, using him to ground herself. Despite the pain, he liked being there for her and taking care of her.

She came when he dragged his tongue upward again and lightly sucked the throbbing bud. Daisy's hands tightened in his hair, but he endured the hint of pain as she sobbed and trembled until her arms went slack, and she collapsed against the bed.

Giving her time to rest before another orgasm, he moved his mouth to the side, finding the scent gland on her right thigh. He licked and nuzzled it as her pheromones drenched him. Slick rushed from her, and he growled his pleasure at proof of what he could do to her. He hoped it equaled the intensity of the effect she had on him.

"Ryder, I need..." She shook her head, looking unsure.

"More pleasure." He grinned and winked before tearing himself from the area of her scent gland and renewing his delicate assault on her sensitive tissue. His tongue was an eager invader, moving with more force this time, since he couldn't hold back. He wanted to feel her come in his mouth again, to taste her juices on his tongue before he plunged his cock inside her.

Just the thought of doing so had him pressing his cock to the bed to apply much-needed pressure to keep his control in check. He wouldn't take her again until she'd come at least once more. With that goal in mind, he licked and sucked until she was crying out her bliss moments later. Her hips pumped aggressively as she pressed her pelvis to his face. He grinned at the way her thighs tightened around him possessively, clearly not wanting to ever let him go.

He was fine with that.

Unable to hold back any longer, Ryder moved up her body and lifted one of her thighs to wrap around his waist. He felt between them to grasp his cock and line it up with her opening. She was wet and ready, but he had a hint of doubt that she could accommodate his size. She'd done so earlier, in estrus, but they were built for each other during that phase. He briefly worried now that she couldn't take him, but her hips lifted even as he paused, wondering if he should make her come once more before trying to enter her.

Her sheath enfolding him banished any questions as he slipped inside easily. He wouldn't last long with how good she felt, and he surrendered his control. He thrust forcefully and rapidly, but she kept pace. Soon, they were moaning together, and the base of his spine tingled as his testicles tightened.

As he surged into her once more, his gaze locked with hers. She seemed lost in the haze of passion, so he hoped she was aware enough of what he was telling her when he said, "I'm going to claim you. You're my Omega, and I'm keeping you."

He dipped his head, skimming back his lips to reveal his teeth. He waited a long moment, giving her a chance to pull away or tell him no. Even though he had every intention of claiming her, he would never force her to accept his bite. If she didn't consent, he would find the strength to hold back until he could convince her she was safe as his Omega, and he would take care of her in every way that mattered.

Instead of protesting, all she did was drag her fingers through his hair and pull his head down while she purred against him. Her sounds of pleasure, combined with the squeezing grasp of her sheath around his shaft while she came yet again, spurred him on.

His cock started to spasm as another orgasm hit him, and he scraped his teeth against her scent gland. She moaned, a low, throaty sound of ecstasy, and his teeth penetrated her skin. There was a sharp taste of copper he found unpleasant, but it quickly faded as her pheromones flooded his olfactory senses, and his world became nothing but the Omega beneath him, clinging to him and milking his cock as he imparted his scent, fusing them together and claiming her as his.

When it was over, he rolled over to his side, taking her with him. They weren't joined by his knot, since she hadn't entered estrus, and he hadn't been rutting, but they were still locked together because he kept her that way. He couldn't bear to pull out from her yet.

He pressed a careful kiss to her forehead as he squeezed her in a light embrace. "My Omega." He sounded fiercely possessive when he said that, and he grinned, enjoying the feeling sweeping through him. She belonged to him now, but he belonged to her just as much.

"My Alpha," she said with obvious satisfaction. She was clearly as pleased as he was. Silence settled between them for a few minutes before she lifted her head slightly so she could look in his eyes. She giggled. "Or should I say Spud?"

He groaned. "Never say that."

She tapped her fingers on his chest. "Tell me how you got the nickname?"

He considered ignoring the request, but she was looking at him with such curiosity, and her expression was so open, that he couldn't bring himself to deny her anything, even if it meant his humiliation. "Quinn and I grew up as part of an orphan clan after our parents died when we were little. They were part of a new colony and picked up Tycho pox. It wiped out a good part of the adults and a few kids. No one came running to check on the survivors, so we had to fend for ourselves."

Her brow furrowed, and she looked at him with obvious sympathy. "I'm so sorry."

He swallowed and looked away for a moment, blinking. Whether it was lucky or unlucky, he barely remembered his folks, so he mourned the absence of memory rather than the people themselves.

He cleared his throat. "Life was rough, and there was a hierarchy. We didn't get enough to eat a lot of times, but one day, I found a potato someone else hadn't dug up during harvest. It was full of eyes and going to seed, but I wanted it." He closed his eyes, easily remembering his empty belly that day and the way his mouth had watered as he envisioned how the potato would taste when roasted.

She was rubbing his arm now, not asking questions. She seemed unable to as she eyed him with compassion.

"An older boy jumped me when I was almost home. He tried to take the potato, but I was determined it was mine. I fought him and beat the sh...stuff out of him. Quinn interceded and pulled me off him, sending Dicky running away. Even then, Quinn was enormous, but I'd held my own. Quinn teased me something awful about how much I was willing to go through for that potato—and I still shared it with him. Somehow, Spud stuck."

She was blinking rapidly and started to sniffle.

He frowned. "What's wrong?"

Daisy sniffed again before answering. "I thought it would be a happier, funnier memory. That makes me feel awful and want to cry."

His chest compressed as the urge to weep hit him for a moment as well. It wasn't because of the memory of that awful time, but from the proof of the care and concern of which his Omega was capable. He cleared his throat. "It was hard, but I survived. Quinn did too."

She drew in a shaky breath, and her expression was still serious when she finally broke her silence a short time later. "What happens now, Ryder?"

He hesitated for a moment. "Just because I'm an Alpha doesn't mean I have all the answers. We'll be together, but I don't know where we're going next. We have to make some money, but I'm loath to risk you by getting back into rathium smuggling."

"I need to return to the convent."

His heart skipped a beat, and he couldn't fight back a fierce wave of anger that swept over him. He turned away from her, breaking the connection between them, as he struggled to control his temper. He didn't want to lash out at her or frighten her. "I already said you belong with me. I can't be without you now that we have a bond established."

The bed squeaked as she moved, and he tensed a moment later when her hands ran down his shoulders before starting to lightly massage his back. "I didn't mean alone. I want you to come with me."

He looked over his shoulder at her, unable to hide his skepticism. "What am I, an Alpha, going to do at an Omega convent? No one else would want me there, even though we're bonded."

She shrugged her shoulder. "I don't plan to stay, but I'd like to know more about my origins. My mother left me there when I was just three, and I have vague memories of her." She shuddered.

He relaxed against her hands. "Good memories?" He didn't think so from her reaction.

"No, but there's a shadowy memory that comes to mind whenever I think of her. I can't make out any of the details anymore, and I don't even know if it's a male or female, but there's someone in my memories who gives me warm feelings, and I'd like to find that person. It might be my father, or perhaps it was my mother's lover. I don't know, but I want to see if I can find them. Now that I have you to keep me safe from other Alphas, I can leave Paladin and explore the galaxy, including finding my origins. Will you help me?"

He melted at the sweet tone she used, trying not to reveal he would help her do anything. She probably already realized he was firmly wrapped around her finger, and he'd move the alignment of the stars if it would make her happy, but he didn't need to reveal that so bluntly. "Of course, I'll help you." As he said that, she embraced him again, her breasts pressing against his back, and he realized he was up for another round of making love to his Omega.

SOMETIME LATER, AFTER they had slept and showered, the computer buzzed to indicate there was an incoming communiqué. They were in the mess hall eating, but he bypassed his wrist comm to have the computer filter the call through the nearest wall monitor. "What's up, Quinn?" He trailed off as he realized it wasn't Quinn in the picture. "I don't think we've met. You must be Azaria."

Her face seemed flushed, though her warm brown complexion made it difficult to discern. She appeared embarrassed though, and he realized maybe she was awkward about the fact he'd seen her naked and in such a state. He struggled to appear nonthreatening as he gave her a smile. "Daisy is right here with me."

Her relief was palpable, and she turned her attention to Daisy as his Omega crowded into the frame with him, smiling at her friend. Azaria looked upset, and Ryder wondered if Quinn had something to do with that.

"Let's go home, Daisy."

Daisy tensed for a moment, but then she nodded. "We were planning to return to Paladin. Before we left, we were going to check in to see if you wanted to come with us." Daisy seemed almost sad that her friend was choosing to do so.

Azaria apparently had no doubts though. "I can't wait to get home."

"I'll bring our ship alongside and use the pincer arm to help you in," said Ryder, eyeing her with some trepidation. He wished he knew what had happened between her and his brother, but whatever it was, it clearly hadn't led to a more permanent connection like he'd found with Daisy. He was sad for his brother, though he understood why Quinn might be resistant to such a bond. Perhaps Azaria had been equally resistant.

With a sigh, he moved away from the comm so he could go to the command room. Soon enough, he had the ship program the coordinates to line up with the cargo bay on his brother's freighter, and the pincer arm was in position when the door opened a few moments later, and Azaria stepped out in an E-suit. She grabbed onto the arm as it wrapped around her, pulling her slowly into the *Remedy* and away from the *Catriona.*

When she was on board, Quinn's cargo door shut, and Ryder accepted the incoming hail. "Is everything okay, Quinn?"

Quinn's expression revealed nothing. "It's fine. I helped her as much as I could, but now she's ready to go home."

Ryder accepted that, knowing he had no right to pry, and from Quinn's closed expression, his brother wasn't going to discuss the situation anyway. Instead, he said, "Thanks again. I'll make sure she gets home safely."

Quinn's features spasmed for a moment, revealing the depth of his concern, which left Ryder puzzled how he could bear to send her away. "See that you do, Spud." With those words, Quinn disconnected the communication between them, and his ship soon veered away from them previous to entering ionospace.

Daisy and Azaria returned to the command deck a few minutes later, and he held out his hand to formally meet her.

"Azaria Khalid, this is Ryder Strang."

Azaria's nostrils flared as her eyes widened, and then she looked at Ryder with something akin to accusation instead of taking his hand. "You claimed her. You selfish bastard."

"It wasn't like that," said Daisy before Ryder could defend himself. She put herself between her friend and him, as though he needed to be protected from the brunette Omega. He struggled not to smile, not wanting either of them to think he was mocking the gesture.

"I chose him, and he chose me. He gave me the option every step of the way. There was nothing coerced about it, okay, Azaria?"

After a moment, and her friend regarding both of them with suspicion, her features relaxed, and she exhaled slowly. "I believe you. I know you wouldn't do anything you don't agree with, unless you got trapped into it." She still seemed to bear a little bit of distrust as she glared at him for a moment before her expression lightened when she looked at Daisy again. "I'm surprised you're returning to Paladin then. As a mated Omega, what will you do there?"

Daisy hesitated and then shrugged. "I don't plan to stay long. I'm sorry, but I have the opportunity to explore now, and I'd like to find out who in my memory leaves such a warm impression."

Azaria's expression softened further, and she clearly knew to whom Daisy referred. "I can't imagine Mother Risa will deny you access to your records, so hopefully you'll find what you're looking for."

With a meaningful glance at Ryder, Daisy looked at him warmly for a long moment before the turning her attention back to her friend. "I suspect I already have, Azaria."

Her words filled Ryder with a strange sense of euphoria, and his chest felt like it might burst from the overflow of emotion. Was he already in love with his Omega? Had it been predestined right from the start, and he'd simply fallen in line with fate's plans?

Normally, he would've chafed at such a thought, but with her, it felt so right that he couldn't question the concept, though he wasn't one for believing in predetermined anything. With her, everything fit together and made sense, and he was thankful for whatever had brought them together, whether it was fate or an accident.

Chapter Seven

THEY ARRIVED AT THE convent's planet a few hours later, and he was impressed by how well it was hidden on the map. It'd taken specific coordinates from Azaria that Daisy had never bothered to memorize, assuming she'd never leave the planet, to get them even in the right quadrant. Then there was a sophisticated system they had to get through, though he noticed signs of damage.

"That must be from when the Klinoks invaded. I don't know how they knew we were here, but it must have seemed like a treasure trove to them," said Azaria with clear bitterness.

"They weren't expecting much resistance," said Daisy with a small smile. It faded to a frown as she shot her friend a look. "I'm so sorry I got us both captured."

Ryder frowned. "I hardly think it was your fault, Daisy."

She smiled at him as she patted his knee. She was perched on his lap, and it still wasn't close enough, but it was all the bounds of propriety would allow with their guest also in the command room. Azaria sat in the copilot seat, determinedly looking away from how close they cuddled.

"That's sweet of you to defend me, but it really was my fault. I've never paid much attention to defense, and I did exactly the wrong thing. Instead of running for the shelter at the convent, I ran deeper into the rooms, and it didn't take them long to find me. Azaria came to rescue me, but there were too many of them, and we were both overwhelmed. I'm going to make sure I learn more about protecting myself."

He growled low in his throat, resisting the urge to remind her that was his job now. It couldn't hurt for her to learn to defend herself, though he couldn't imagine a situation where she would ever be alone and have to, short of his death. "I'll show you some things."

She smiled at him again, clearly approving of the idea. "Thank you, love."

It was a simple endearment, but it threatened to turn his whole body into a pile of goo, and he almost purred again. He wasn't certain how Azaria would react to his purring, so he kept it to himself, though he squeezed Daisy's thigh in his hand a little firmer before loosening his hold slightly.

"You're entering restricted space. Turn around before you're blown out of the sky," said a real voice through the computer.

"Mother Risa, it's us," said Azaria. "Daisy and me...and her Alpha." She sounded unhappy as she tacked on the last part.

There was silence, and then a woman's face appeared before him. He had expected her to be quite a bit older, since she was obviously the leader of the convent, but she couldn't have been much more than a few years past forty. She had a surprisingly fresh face and blonde hair with nary a strand of gray, but there was an uncompromising hardness in her features that put him on edge.

"What Alpha?"

"Me," said Ryder with a hint of protectiveness as he pulled Daisy tighter against him. "Daisy wants to know more about her origin so we can find her family, if she has some."

"And I just want to come home," said Azaria.

The woman seemed like she might reject them for a moment, but then she sighed and nodded. "I'll allow the security protocols to give you entrance, but your ship will be immediately locked down once you land. Do you accept those terms, Alpha?" Her voice dripped with disdain.

"I accept as long as everyone realizes I won't tolerate any signs of aggression or attempts to hurt my mate."

Her eyes widened. "Daisy was once one of us. No one would hurt her."

He felt Daisy stiffen against him, and he rubbed her thigh in a soothing fashion. "I accept your terms then."

The screen went dark without Mother Risa saying another word, and Daisy was clearly tense and unhappy on his lap.

"She talks like I'm not welcome there anymore." She sniffed lightly.

"It's not that you aren't welcome, but you aren't really one of us anymore." Azaria sounded apologetic as she reached out to take Daisy's hand, squeezing lightly. "You aren't running away from Alphas or seeking protection from them now. You have your own to keep you safe, and you have to admit, it's a security risk for you and an Alpha to know where we are."

Daisy scowled. "I would never reveal that to anyone."

Ryder stiffened his spine as well. "Neither would I. I respect what you're doing here, and I believe you all have the right to make the decision that's best for you."

Azaria seemed to accept and believe his words. She nodded and released her hand. Daisy sagged against her mate, obviously still sad at her change in status among the women she'd grown up with, but she was soon cuddling closer. He hoped she wouldn't regret accepting his claim, and with the way she curled against him, purring softly, he couldn't imagine she would. She seemed as happy as him that they'd found each other.

Chapter Eight

RYDER WAS QUITE AN anomaly, and she knew some of the women on the planet had never seen an Alpha. Their responses were somewhere between open hostility and blatant curiosity, though most of them just tended to stay out of his way as they all sat down for dinner.

It was a quiet, subdued affair, and she was used to it being more boisterous and filled with conversation. Ryder's presence definitely stifled them, and she had a new appreciation for why Mother Risa no longer considered her one of them. Now that her other half was Ryder, his presence had to be considered as well. He would have an inhibitive effect on the sisters, and she didn't want that.

With that in mind, she said to Mother Risa, "We plan to leave in the morning. I'd like to see what data you have about me."

Mother Risa nodded. "Of course. Once dinner is finished, I'll take you into the office and share what information your mother left about you." She sent Ryder a look, as though feeling defensive. "I would've given that information to Daisy any time she asked. I'm not trying to hide the truth from these women."

If Ryder had considered that, he didn't show it. "I didn't think you were, Mother Risa. The women don't seem afraid or coerced to stay here. I do worry they might be hearing some untrue things about Alphas though." He frowned.

The mother scowled. "What might be untrue, Alpha...Mr. Strang?"

Daisy looked at Ryder, taking his hand in a silent reminder not to be too harsh or assertive. He nodded at her once before looking at Risa. "I'm afraid they think all Alphas are selfish, bestial sex machines, who only want one thing and will do anything to take it. Some are like that, but not all."

Risa sniffed. "I shall have to take your word for it, Mr. Strang. From what I've heard, the first assessment is far more accurate. Ones who are supposedly like you are far rarer than the other kind."

His eyes widened, and Daisy opened her mouth, prepared to intercede. She didn't want Mother Risa sending them away from the planet before she had a chance to learn more about her family.

It was unnecessary though. Ryder said, "I only know what I've experienced myself, but I know several decent Alphas, my brother among them. I met a man recently who was an incredibly good Alpha to his Omega, Maya. They had a child, a little girl, and it was obvious he would've died to protect her too."

Risa's eyes widened slightly. "As I said, I'll defer to you on the assertion. I haven't met any besides you."

His eyes widened. "You've never met Alphas besides me?"

She shrugged a shoulder. "Why would I have? My mother was a founding member of the convent, and I've never left Paladin. I've never wished to."

Ryder let out a sound that was similar to choking, and Daisy gave him a repressive look. His lips twitched for a moment, but he didn't say anything more. He just finished his meal quietly, and she was relieved when they were done eating, and Risa had finished as well.

When she rose, they got up and followed her from the dining hall through the hallways of the convent to her office. She gestured for them to sit in front of her desk as she moved to a wall of microdisks, using A.I. to call up Daisy's. Less than a minute later, she presented a small chip to Daisy. "This is everything I know about your origins. I hope it helps you find what you're looking for, Daisy."

Daisy sensed it was time for them to leave, and she knew everyone at the convent would rest easier if they weren't there. They would sleep on the ship for tonight before heading out in the morning. At least, that was her plan unless Ryder had a reason not to.

She stood up, moving over to Mother Superior and hugging her spontaneously. "Thank you for everything, Mother Risa."

Risa looked like she might cry for a moment as well. Her eyes blinked rapidly, but then she regained control. She smoothed curls off Daisy's face and cupped her cheek lightly for a moment before saying, "It was a pleasure to have you here with us. Take care of yourself, dear." She looked at Ryder then, her expression hardening, and her voice stern. "And you take care of her as well."

"I certainly will, Mother Risa." He bowed his head deferentially.

Daisy stepped away from Risa and moved over to Ryder, wrapping her hand around his as they quickly departed the office, and then the convent a few minutes later. Azaria was waiting in the garden as they walked by, and she paused long enough to trade goodbyes with her dear friend. "I hope to see you again, Azaria."

Azaria smiled. "I hope to as well, but I suspect that won't be happening. We'll have to content ourselves with communicating electronically, since I have no plans to leave Paladin, and I think you know you can't come back."

Daisy absorbed the information, though she already knew it, with a stoic nod. "I realize that. I'll miss you."

"I'll miss you too, my friend." Azaria looked over Daisy's shoulder to Ryder. "Thank you for your assistance, Mr. Strang. And thank your brother for me as well." Her expression closed as soon as she mentioned Quinn, and she turned away from them without another word.

Daisy was curious what had happened, but she couldn't push her friend to disclose it, especially under the circumstances. Perhaps when some time had passed, Azaria would feel like confiding in her if she needed an ear and a shoulder, even if it were offered remotely.

Chapter Nine

ONCE THEY WERE ABOARD, Ryder sat down and pulled Daisy onto his lap before pushing the disk into the computer on his ship. It didn't take long for the A.I. to translate the language it was written in and interface, and her file soon appeared.

They scanned it together, gleaning the name of the planet from where she hailed. When he asked the computer to bring up information about it, it turned out to be a small agrarian planet owned by a man named Lucien Collins. He looked at Daisy when she gasped. "What is it?"

"Collins is my last name."

He blinked as he realized he'd never learned it until now. "He might not be any relation."

She nodded, "I know, since it's a common last name, but it's a small planet, so it gives me tenuous hope. Can we please go there?"

He frowned. "Of course we can." He was unlikely to deny her what she most wanted, and he was hurt she had even asked. He reminded himself to restrain the sensitivity, since they still had a period of adjustment until they both realized the depth of their feelings for each other and the extent of their devotion to the other.

They had the bond between Alpha and Omega, but they still had to build another bond, one that was even more intimate and deeper. The loving bond between Ryder and Daisy required more attention and construction than the natural connection forged by their biological imperatives. Though it was well on its way to being established, it was still faltering at the moment.

"I'm suddenly nervous. What if he told her to send me away?" She was nibbling on her lower lip in her anxiety.

He reached up to gently brush the full lip from between her teeth, getting her to stop the nervous habit. "Perhaps he did, but I find it unlikely. You said there's someone in your past who gives you warm feelings. Maybe it's this man. Or someone on the planet."

Her dark-brown eyes were filled with fear. "What if it's not him? What if I get there and find out there's no one left who cares about me?"

He pulled her into his arms, hating the hint of heartbreak in her features. "It's a possibility, but it doesn't mean it's likely. If the worst happens, there's certainly someone who cares about you. You're not alone anymore, and you never will be again as long as there's breath in my body. I will love and care for you 'til the day I die, Daisy."

She pulled back, having stiffened slightly when he used the word love. "What happens if I die first?"

He shrugged a shoulder. "That doesn't mean my devotion will lessen. I've seen firsthand how an Alpha can continue loving an Omega even after he loses her. That will be me if something happens to you, but I can't imagine that. Whatever might take you has to get through me first."

She started to giggle, even as her eyes flooded with tears. "That's exceedingly morbid, but I find comfort in it."

"Then I've done my job as your Alpha." He purred lightly, which seemed to soothe her, and she was soon napping in his arms. It was only after she'd fallen asleep that he realized she'd never reciprocated or told him she loved him.

He tried not to panic or worry about that. Their relationship was still new, just blossoming, and though he might be certain of his feelings for her, she needed time and deserved the right and respect to discover her own for him without being rushed into something.

Chapter Ten

THE JOURNEY SEEMED to take forever, though it was only a few hours once they set out from Paladin. When they reached the planet, there was no sophisticated security system like there'd been to hide Paladin's presence, but it was still a challenge to get through. Ryder was currently in conversation with a third flight control officer after the first two hadn't yielded, trying to persuade her to allow a landing.

"I'm afraid I can't authorize you to land, Captain Strang. We've had some thefts on the planet, so we've locked down security. Only authorized visitors and merchant transporters are allowed on or off." Her face was stern, and her decision was clearly made.

Daisy stopped pacing, leaning over Ryder's shoulder to look at the flight control officer. "I'd like to speak to Lucien Collins please." She was acting strictly on instinct.

The woman's expression didn't change. "And who are you?"

"My name is Daisy Collins." She licked her lips. "I think Lucien Collins is my father."

The flight control officer looked skeptical, but apparently, she didn't want to completely discount the idea and risk being disciplined. "Hold the line and stay in hover mode." She disappeared from the monitor a moment later.

Ryder took her hand, pulling her onto his lap to stop her ceaseless pacing. "Calm down, honey. Whatever happens, it's okay."

She nodded, unable to verbally express just how nervous she was. She was on the cusp of knowing more about herself, of understanding how she'd ended up at the convent, but that was all predicated on if she was truly related to someone on the planet, or if she could even get permission to set down to find out.

The flight control officer reappeared a moment later, and though her expression was still impassive, she looked a little less frigid. "Follow the coordinates I'm sending and land there immediately. Your weapons will be rendered neutral while you're visiting the planet." She disappeared from the screen.

"That's maybe a good sign," said Ryder encouragingly. He squeezed her hand before gently moving her to the copilot's seat so he could program the computer to follow the coordinates relayed to them from flight control below.

Daisy sat there, nails digging into the upholstery of the seat as she anticipated a possible reunion with someone who might know or her care about her. It was amazing to have Ryder, and she'd never expected to find an Alpha of her own that she felt safe and content with, but there was still a part of her missing. The idea it might soon be filled was tantalizing, and it left her head spinning, even as her stomach twisted into knots from anxiety.

The *Remedy* sat down moments later, and Ryder frowned. "The weapons have been neutralized." He sounded a little unhappy about that, but he didn't appear overly fearful. He stood up, and he was the same confident man he always was when he took her arm and pulled her against him gently, giving her an encouraging side-hug. "Remember, we'll get through it together, whether it's good or bad."

She managed to smile, though she was still feeling sick as they went to the cargo bay. The atmosphere on the planet was fine, having likely been terraformed long ago, so they didn't require an E-suit. It was nice to step outside and feel real breeze running through her hair again after having been confined to the ship and in the box. The convent had been the same old, same old, but this felt new and different, yet somehow familiar.

She looked around at the endless expanses of golden fields, and an image came to her mind of a pair of steady black hands, much larger than hers, holding a sprout for her to examine and telling her in a calm, deep voice how to plant the seedling to keep it alive.

She was trembling as she walked down the gangplank. When her feet stepped onto the dust, it blew around and made her sneeze, but even that wasn't unpleasant.

As she took a few steps forward, a big black man suddenly appeared in front of her. He had curly silver hair and a neatly trimmed beard, and his size and breadth revealed he was an Alpha. He was an intimidating sight, especially as he rushed toward her. She was frozen in fear for a moment before her feet remembered how to function, and she took a cautious pace forward, disengaging from Ryder with an apologetic look. He didn't seem to mind as she took a couple of hesitant steps toward the man rushing toward her.

He didn't stop to shake her hand. Instead, he swept her into his arms and hugged her tightly, and as he did so, a wave of longing and familiarity swept over her. She recognized his scent, recalling his cologne mixed with the sweat of labor as they'd worked side-by-side more than once in the fields while he'd tried to teach her everything he could. Her memories went back that far, and the figure in her mind started to coalesce as she realized it was this man whose arms were around her.

"My dear, sweet Daisy. I never thought I'd see you again." There was genuine anguish in his tone, and he seemed to find it difficult to pull back and let go of her even fractionally. His hands remained on her shoulders, and he stared down at her avidly.

Daisy was staring up at him just as keenly, seeing several similarities between them. They had the same nose, though hers was smaller and more delicate. His eyes were more slanted than hers, but they were the same shade. They had the same lips as well, though their ears were completely differently shaped.

He had a high and noble brow, and he seemed regal like a king, though there was a heaviness to his posture. Yet it seemed to lighten the longer he stared at her. "How did you ever find your way back, Daisy?"

Ryder stepped forward then, and there was a hint of protectiveness about him, though he did nothing more than take Daisy's hand, which she clung to. "I think the more important question is, how did she ever lose her way from you to start with, sir?"

Her father growled for a moment, facing Ryder, then one of his hands dropped away from her shoulder. The other remained, holding her gently as he faced off with her Alpha. "That's a long story, so explain to me why I should share it with you?"

"He's my Alpha," said Daisy firmly, moving between them and leaning against Ryder in an effort to prevent any hostilities. "He would never harm me, but he wants to make sure I'm safe. I think it's a story we both need to hear, sir."

"Call me Papa."

As he said the words, she vaguely remembered the times she had run through the fields, shouting "Papa" at the top of her lungs in joy as she looked for him. She shivered as she remembered an incident where a shadowy figure had found her instead, dragging her into the house and whipping her. She shuddered, certain that figure wasn't the man in her memory, but not sure who it was.

"Come up to the house, and we'll have some refreshments and a discussion." He seemed reluctant to release her, but he finally did, taking a step back and walking ahead of them.

Daisy and Ryder exchanged a glance, and she gave him a smile of reassurance. "I think he's the man from my memory," she said softly.

He still appeared wary, but he relaxed marginally as he nodded at her. "In that case, I'm prepared to hear what he says."

Minutes later, they were seated outside at a patio that afforded a glimpse of the entire farmland around them. "It's huge."

Lucien smiled at her comment and nodded as he poured them both a glass of some ice-cold beverage. "It is. There are a few other families, but most of this belongs to us."

Daisy shifted with discomfort, hoping he didn't mean her in the *us*. It didn't feel right to lay claim to any of this since she hadn't grown up here.

"What happened to Daisy all those years ago?"

Her father sighed as he leaned back, pushing hair off his face. "I had a woman for a while, a Beta, named Omalla. It was a mutually beneficial arrangement." He appeared to flush as he made the admission, shooting Daisy an apologetic look. "I certainly didn't expect to have a child with her. I'm sure you're aware how difficult it can be for Betas and Alphas to procreate successfully."

Daisy nodded.

"I had been prepared to send Omalla on her way before she revealed her news. She was always a little unstable, so I wasn't entirely convinced I believed her. I kept her here on the farm until she was far enough along for the doctor to confirm you were my child. After that, I married her."

He heaved a sigh as he closed his eyes for a long moment before opening them again. "It was one of the worst mistakes I ever made, but I thought I was doing the right thing. She was jealous of everyone and everything, and she was particularly awful to you, especially if I paid any attention to you. I didn't let that stop me, and I soon had her confined to her own home on the other side of the farm.

"She had companions whose task it was to keep her in line, but she occasionally still slipped away. When she did, she was horrible to you. The last time she was alone with you, she beat you, and I nearly beat her myself. Only you calling for me to comfort you held me back, and I ordered her banished from the planet. It wasn't what I wanted to do. I wanted to destroy her, and heaven help me, but I wish I had."

Daisy wasn't unmoved by his sadness, and she reached over to touch his hand lightly. "I think I remember her sometimes. She was a dark and shadowy figure in my life, and whenever I think of her, I feel fear."

"That sounds like Omalla." His mouth twisted bitterly, as though her name were something foul to taste. "Things were relatively quiet for the next few days as they prepared for her departure. I wanted nothing to do with her or even to know where she was going. I told my people to arrange it so she was somewhere she would be safe, and others would be safe from her, especially you.

"At the last moment, she slipped away from them and took you. She left in the middle of the night on an old ship that never should have left the planet, bringing you along with her, but I had no idea where she took you. Until today, I feared she had simply killed you as a way to hurt me. She claimed that when I caught up with her, but part of me could never give up hope."

Daisy's mouth trembled for a moment, and she struggled not to cry when she realized just how much her own mother had hated her. It didn't mitigate the pain to know her mother might've been unwell and unable to make herself love anyone. It still hurt deeply, and she blinked back tears as Ryder squeezed her hand.

"Where did you end up, my dear?" Lucien took a moment to wipe his eyes before he looked at her again. "Whoever helped take care of you, I owe them a great debt."

"She took me to a convent for Omegas. I'm not sure she realized what it was exactly, since the ship she was in malfunctioned. The farmers on a nearby moon helped her get to the planet, since they didn't have room for outsiders. According to the records, we stayed a couple of days while one of the sisters repaired the ship. The information is vague on how she did it, but Mother Risa was able to convince her to leave me there."

Unfortunately, the records had been a little hazy, so she had no way to know if her mother had accidentally stumbled across Paladin, or if she'd been intentionally seeking it. From what she'd heard of Omalla already and remembered of her, she had a difficult time believing her mother had benignly left her there, or that had been her intent at the beginning anyway.

Her father blinked, seeming to absorb the information for a moment. "I don't know what made her find that hint of kindness, but I'm grateful for it."

Unconvinced it was kindness and not just a stroke of luck, combined with the perceptiveness of Mother Risa in realizing Omalla wasn't motherly toward her helpless child, she didn't agree or disagree. "What happened to her?" asked Daisy as she prepared herself to hear the worst. She expected her father to confess to having killed Omalla, and though she couldn't entirely blame him if he had, it was still a frightening prospect.

He shrugged. "I don't really know all the details. After I caught up with her and realized she no longer had you, I was done with her. I provided nothing else for her. I severed the marriage within weeks, and it only took that long because of legalities.

"I have no idea what happened to her in the interim, but five years ago, I was called by some ineffectual official on a backwater planet at the ass-end of the galaxy. She'd gotten into a bar fight and was stabbed seventeen times. Obviously, she didn't survive. They expected me to claim her body and bury her, but I told them to dump her in the nearest pauper's grave."

He winced slightly. "I apologize for being so blunt, daughter, but I couldn't care less what happened to her or her remains. If you wish to track her down, I probably have the information somewhere in my records. Likely, she's still buried on that planet."

Ryder's arms tightly around her as he pulled her closer for comfort when Daisy shivered. She shook her head. "I don't care to find her." Knowing what had happened to her mother provided plenty of closure, especially the more she considered just how Omalla had wronged her and Lucien.

It was clear her father loved her and had her entire life. He was the warm, soothing presence she remembered, and he had stayed with her though she'd only been three the last time she saw him. Her mother had taken her away from him, denying her the life she should've had while breaking her father's heart, leaving him in anguish to never know exactly what had happened to his child. Hatred filled her, and she was glad her father had turned his back on any responsibility to the woman. She deserved to molder in an unmarked grave on some remote planet.

"You're here now, and we have to focus on the present, not the past." His heavy expression gradually faded to a grin. "You must stay. There's plenty of room, and I'd be happy to have both of you. I'd like to get to know your young man."

Daisy stiffened slightly, looking at Ryder. After a moment, he nodded. She turned back to her father with a smile. "We'd be pleased to stay."

"In that case, I'll have Sharinda show you to a room. Dinner will be served in a couple of hours, so that gives you time to rest and recover from your journey. I look forward to hearing about your life and getting to know you again." Lucien reached out to grasp her fingers in a tight grip.

Daisy squeezed back with just as much fervor. "I'm excited as well, Papa." Perhaps it should've been too soon, but as she said the word, it felt completely right. Whatever had been missing felt like it was starting to fill in, and she was riding high on a tide of jubilation as she followed his housekeeper up the stairs a short time later with Ryder right behind her.

Once they were in their new quarters, she turned to face her lover. "It's amazing. I was afraid it was going to be horrible, but this is the best thing that could happen."

Ryder smiled, but he seemed concerned. He turned away from her as he nodded. "Yes, it's wonderful."

With a frown, she moved closer, putting her hand on his shoulder and getting him to turn back to her. "Why don't I believe you?"

He flashed a ghost of a smile. "I guess I'm just worried I'll be superfluous. You've found where you belong, and I could never imagine staying on one planet forever. You're my Omega, but I'm afraid I've just lost you."

She couldn't help it. Daisy giggled. His expression tightened, so she did her best to stifle the initial reaction of amusement. Instead, she cupped his face in her hands and stretched on her tiptoes, brushing her mouth against his. "You haven't lost me. We'll stay for a while, but I want to go too. I want to see all the things I've missed, being protected as I was on Paladin. We still want the same things, and I love you. I don't want you to leave without me. I feel like we were meant to find each other, and nothing's going to pull us apart now. I want to get to know my father and stay for a while, but that doesn't mean we have to live here."

He looked relieved, and then he pulled her into his arms. "I feel like I'm being a selfish Alpha. I should be able to set aside the reluctance to stay in one place if that's what you want. If this is what you decide you need, I'll find a way to make it work."

"I appreciate that, but I think we should have a partnership. Neither of us should be sacrificing too much to make the other happy. We should find options that make us both happy." She leaned forward, kissing him again, this time drawing it into a long, slow embrace that left them both breathless when they parted several minutes later. "There's a whole world waiting for us to explore together. Don't lose faith in us now."

After a moment, Ryder nodded, and he looked far more confident. "I suppose it was just an instant of doubt anyway. Our relationship is so new and still forming, and you don't need me now."

She scowled at him as she pressed her fingers to his lips. "Watch what you say before you make me angry. I still need you. You're my Alpha, and I'm your Omega. I suspect you're the ideal for me and vice versa. No matter what else happens, or what we find or go through, we're still going to have this bond between us. It will be ever-deepening. Don't you agree?"

He nodded emphatically. "Yes, and I hate that I'm revealing any misgivings. I don't doubt the strength of our bond and the love we're forming. I guess I'm just scared to lose you."

"Perhaps you aren't supposed to be afraid, since you're an Alpha, but I like seeing this side of you. I don't enjoy your fear, but I like knowing there's vulnerability in you. It makes me love you even more." She brushed her mouth against his cheek. "I have a feeling I'll love you even more tomorrow." She kissed him on the other cheek. "And even more next year." She brushed her lips against his. "And beyond the bounds of imagining in the years to come."

"I'm sure you're right." His mouth took possession of hers then, and there was no gentle brushing or quickly darting away. This was a serious, intense kiss full of promises and passion, and she had no interest in breaking it.

When it naturally led to the two of them sprawling on the bed, sharing their passion and love in a more physical way, Daisy felt only reassured and complete as they joined. Her future seemed unexpectedly brighter than she'd ever imagined, and she looked forward to seeing what each day brought with her Alpha beside her.

DID YOU MISS THE FIRST book in the Galactic Alphas series? "Alpha's Omega" starts it all, and finish off the series with Azaria and Quinn's story, "Claiming His Omega."

About Juno

JUNO WELLS GREW UP on Florida's Space Coast, watching the shuttles take off from Cape Canaveral. When she hit college, her childhood fantasies about space travel turned highly romantic. Now her mind reels with space adventures of fantastic alien lords in distant galaxies, and the Earth women they love.

Wells' stories explore the complex, sensual relationships between inhabitants of different star systems. There are always happy endings just as there is always a new world to explore.

Did you love *Buying His Omega*? Then you should read *Claiming His Omega*[1] by Juno Wells!

Azaria and Daisy were both kidnapped from their Omega convent and sold at a Klinok auction. The two are separated, sold to different buyers, with Daisy landing in a good situation. Daisy's Alpha, Ryder, helps rescue Azaria, and after Quinn Strang assists Azaria during her forced estrus at his brother's request, they go their separate ways. She doesn't expect to see him again, but when the gangster who originally bought her tracks her to Paladin, she has no choice but to call him for help.Quinn recruits his brother and Ryder's friend, Remy, to help rescue the Omega he walked away from weeks ago. He hasn't stopped thinking about her, and once he rescues her from Aldrich Garros, he's going to

---

1. https://books2read.com/u/mqr6kZ

2. https://books2read.com/u/mqr6kZ

do what he should have done then—claim her despite all the reasons he didn't the first time.

Also by Juno Wells

Alien Baby Pact
Baby For The Brundle Commander
Baby For The Grimlock General
Baby For The Palantir Chief
Baby For The Alphan Captain

Dazon Agenda
Written In The Stars
Alien's Babies
Diplomatic Affairs
Moon Madness
Across The Stars
Emperor's Assassin Bride
Dazon Agenda: Complete Collection

Galactic Alphas
Alpha's Omega
Buying His Omega
Claiming His Omega
Galactic Alphas Compilation

Standalone
Alien General's Rebel Consort